WITHDRAWN
Anne Arundel Co Public Library

Rum Pum Pum

by David L. Harrison and Jane Yolen

Illustrated by Anjan Sarkar

HOLIDAY HOUSE  NEW YORK

To JY for inviting me to play; to GM for saying, "Yes," which in editor talk means, "If you are walking on this fine day, I will come, too"; and to JH, here at last is your tiger story.—DLH

To DLH for his willingness to play, and to GM who made us play harder—JY

To Barbara and Paresh (aka Mum & Dad!)—AS

Printed and bound in April 2020 at Toppan Leefung, DonGuan City, China.

The artwork was created with digital paint, colored pencils, and lino print texture.

www.holidayhouse.com

First Edition

1 3 5 7 9 10 8 6 4 2

Library of Congress Cataloging-in-Publication Data

Names: Harrison, David L. (David Lee), 1937- author. | Yolen, Jane, author. | Sarkar, Anjan, illustrator.

Title: Rum pum pum / by David L. Harrison and Jane Yolen ; illustrated by Anjan Sarkar.

Description: First edition. | New York : Holiday House, [2020] | Audience: Ages 4–8. | Audience: Grades K–1.

Summary: "'Rrrrh!' means 'Let's be friends' in tiger talk, but the other animals don't understand him and run away! Maybe the gentle 'rum-pum-pum' of the drum can help him find a friend"—Provided by publisher. | Identifiers: LCCN 2019039805 | ISBN 9780823441006 (hardcover)

Subjects: CYAC: Tigers—Fiction. | Jungle animals—Fiction. | Drum—Fiction. | Friendship—Fiction. | Animal communication—Fiction. Animal sounds—Fiction. | Classification: LCC PZ7.H2474 Ru 2020 | DDC [E]—dc23

LC record available at https://lccn.loc.gov/2019039805

There once was a tiger,
a large, handsome tiger
with sharp claws,
big, sharp teeth,
and a long, sinuous tail.
But he had no friends.

Tiger wandered around the forest
saying "*Rrrrrrrrrhhh,*"
which in tiger talk means,
"Will you be my friend?"

But whether it was his growl
or his claws or his big, sharp teeth,
everyone he met
immediately ran away.

And then one day
as Tiger strolled a forest path,
he found a strange object
under a sal tree.

He rolled it with his nose.
He licked it with his tongue.

He chewed an edge with his teeth.
He scratched it with his claws.

"*Rrrrrrrrrhhh,*" Tiger said.

When the strange object
did not immediately run away,
Tiger thumped it with his long, sinuous tail.

Suddenly the strange object spoke back.
"*Rum pum pum,*" it said.

Tiger picked up
his brand-new friend,
and they went along
and went along
and went along the road.

Soon they met
a very old monkey swinging
in a mango tree.
Tiger thumped his tail
against his new friend.
"*Rum pum pum,*" said Tiger's friend.
"*Rrrrrrrrrhhh,*" said Tiger.

Monkey chattered,
"*Chee-chee-chee,*"
which in monkey talk means,
"If you are walking on this fine day,
I will come, too.
Though most of the time I will stay
high in the branches until I am sure
I'll be safe on the ground."
She did not get to be that old
without being cautious
and becoming very wise.

"*Rum pum pum,*" said Tiger's friend.
"*Rrrrrrrrrhhh,*" said Tiger.
"*Chee-chee-chee,*" said Monkey.
And they all went along
and went along
and went along the road.

Soon they met
a gray, grumpy rhinoceros
munching grass
by the side of the road.
Tiger thumped his tail
against his new friend.
"*Rum pum pum,*" said Tiger's friend.
"*Rrrrrrrrrhhh,*" said Tiger.
"*Chee-chee-chee,*" said Monkey.

"Ouggggggh!" groused Rhinoceros,
which in rhino talk means,
"This is a fine day for walking.
I will come, too."

And so they all went along
and went along
and went along the road.
Soon they met a green parrot
with a red rump
sunning its wings on a banyan limb.
Tiger thumped his tail
against his new friend.
"*Rum pum pum,*" said Tiger's friend.
"*Rrrrrrrrrhhh,*" said Tiger.
"*Chee-chee-chee,*" said Monkey.
"*Ouggggghh!*" groused Rhinoceros.

"*Scree-awk!*" squawked Parrot,
which in parrot talk means,
"I'm very busy,
but if you are going down that road,
I will come, too."
Parrots are always busy,
and busy-bodies as well.

And so they all went along
and went along
and went along the road.
Soon they met a chameleon
watching a cricket.

Tiger thumped his tail
against his new friend.
"*Rum pum pum,*" said Tiger's friend.
"*Rrrrrrrrrhhh,*" said Tiger.
"*Chee-chee-chee,*" said Monkey.
"*Ouggggggh!*" groused Rhinoceros.
"*Scree-awk!*" squawked Parrot.

Chameleon flicked her long tongue,
which in lizard talk means,
"If you are going down that road,
I will come, too."
Lizards can always be convinced
to try something new.
The cricket was relieved.

And so they all went along
and went along
and went along the road.
Soon they met
a wrinkly-kneed elephant
pulling off leaves
from an ouu tree.
Tiger thumped his tail
against his new friend.

"*Rum pum pum,*" said Tiger's friend.
"*Rrrrrrrrrhhh,*" said Tiger.
"*Chee-chee-chee,*" said Monkey.
"*Ougggggh!*" groused Rhinoceros.
"*Scree-awk!*" squawked Parrot.
Chameleon flicked her long tongue.

"Areeeeeyahhh!" trumpeted Elephant,
which in elephant talk means,
"It's a good day for a walk.
I need to stretch my baggy knees.
If you are going down that road,
I will come, too."

No one argues with Elephant.
So they all went along
and went along
and went along the road.

But after a while,
Rhinoceros groused,
"Why do you, Tiger,
always get to hold Friend?"
Elephant added,
"With my trunk, I could carry Friend
much more easily than you."
"With my beak," squawked Parrot.

“My tongue!” flicked Chameleon.
“My hands OR my feet!” shrieked Monkey.
“I found Friend, that’s why!” Tiger said.
But no one was listening.
They were growling and shouting,
they were squawking and shrieking,
they were flicking and making
so much noise that . . .

. . . a boy came out of the forest
to see what all the fuss was about.
"Oh my," said the boy, pointing.
"You have all found Drum.
I wondered where it went."

He picked it up,
and then he petted it
and he patted it.

He tickled it
and tapped it.

He pounded it
and pummeled it.

And as he did so,
he and Drum told the story
of a large, handsome, lonely tiger,
and how Tiger had at last
found some very good friends
to go along the road with him.

When the story was over,
Tiger and Monkey and Rhinoceros,
Parrot and Chameleon and Elephant
all remembered—they were friends.
And then Tiger said,
"Boy, Drum, tell the story again."

So Boy and Drum told the story
again until everyone fell asleep
in the soft Indian night,
dreaming of going along
and along and along
the winding story road,
all the way till morning.

A Note from
David L. Harrison and Jane Yolen

The trees and animals in this book are all from India, but they aren't all found in the same habitats, though the *ouu* or elephant apple is truly a mainstay of the Indian elephant's diet.

The boy's missing drum is one of a pair of drums that are collectively called *tabla*. The lost and found drum of this story is the smaller one with the higher voice. The drums come from India. Each drum is played by hitting it or touching it or stroking it with one's fingers and palm.

As for Lonely Tiger

A tiger runs faster, leaps higher, and is stronger than most other creatures on Earth. Tigers have been around for three million years or more. One hundred years ago 100,000 tigers roamed throughout Asia. Today only 3,000 to 4,000 tigers are left in the entire world.

Perhaps Tiger really does need help from his friends. Can you think of ways we can help?

Signed, two good friends,

Jane Yolen & David L. Harrison

---

http://www.tigersintheforest.co.uk/save-the-tiger

https://www.nationalgeographic.com/animals/mammals/b/bengal-tiger/

http://www.defenders.org/tiger/basic-facts

http://www.ngkids.co.uk/did-you-know/10-tiger-facts